The FurFins

If you tiptoe to the seashore
and gaze out at the sea,
you might just spot a sparkly tail
or a friendly furry face.
You've just seen a FurFin and found
a very special place.

Shhh, FurFins are real . . .

The FurFins

TinyTail and the Lost Treasure

Written by
ALISON RITCHIE

Illustrated by
ALESS BAYLIS

BLOOMSBURY
CHILDREN'S BOOKS

LONDON OXFORD NEW YORK NEW DELHI SYDNEY

Deep beneath the silvery waves,
nestled in a kaleidoscope of colourful coral,
lies the magical Kingdom of Coralia.
This is where the FurFins live.

There's StarTail's pod with a sparkly star in
the window and – look – that pod over there . . .

the one with the little pink heart on the door,
that belongs to TinyTail and her seahorse, Boo.

"Snapping shrimps!" exclaimed TinyTail excitedly as she swooshed out of her pod. She had some wonderful news and she couldn't wait to share it with Boo.

"Come on, Boo. I know you're here somewhere," she said. "Come out, come out wherever you are. "

The trouble was that Boo loved playing hide-and-seek, and he was VERY good at it.

TinyTail was just wondering where to look next when her friend,
StarTail, came swishing by with her seahorse, Shine.
At last she could share her news!

"Guess what?"
she blurted out.
"I've lost my
first scale!"

Every FurFin got excited about losing their very first scale. If they put the scale
in a special bag and hung it outside their pod at night, the Scale Fairy
would come and replace it with a magical, sparkling new scale.

StarTail smiled. "I remember when my first scale came out. The Scale Fairy
gave me this one. It's got a sparkling crystal star on it!"

TinyTail took her scale from her bag
and showed it to her friend.

"Ooh," said StarTail. "It's a dainty one –
take care not to lose it."

But, just at that very moment . . .

BOO!

Out popped Boo from behind
a big clump of seagrass.

Poor TinyTail got such a surprise
that she somersaulted in the water,
and dropped her tiny scale!

StarTail tried to catch it but it was too late. The scale floated out of sight.

"Now I'll never get it back," sighed TinyTail. "The Scale Fairy won't come and I'll have a scale missing forever."

As a salty tear fell down TinyTail's cheek, Giggle and Hee-hee, the clown fish came by.
"Hey, have you heard this one?" said Giggle, chuckling.
"Why did the lobster blush? . . .

Because the sea weed."

"Get it?" laughed Hee-hee. "Get it? Because the sea weed."
The pair flapped about laughing but then realized that
no one else was joining in with the fun.

When TinyTail explained all about her lost scale, poor Boo hung his head.

"Don't worry, Boo," said StarTail, giving the little seahorse a hug. "We'll find TinyTail's scale, you'll see."

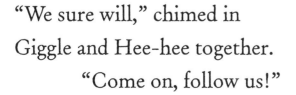

"We sure will," chimed in Giggle and Hee-hee together. "Come on, follow us!"

So Giggle and Hee-hee led the way and they all began the search for TinyTail's scale.

They looked everywhere and asked everyone . . .

from the Sea Urchins . . .

to the Reef Fish . . .

and the Sea Slugs...

to the Shrimps...

but, sadly, TinyTail's scale was nowhere to be found.

Then they came to a HUGE drop in the ocean...

THE BIG DEEP!

Everyone peered over the edge into
the darkness, where the Sharks lived
and where no FurFin dared to go.

"Good luck if you are going down there," said Giggle and Hee-hee,
swishing off. "What does a shark eat for dinner? . . .

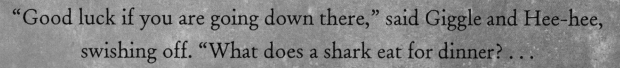

Anything it wants!"

"That's it then," said TinyTail.
"My scale is lost forever."

But StarTail wasn't ready to give up yet.
"Come on, I know what you need – a big hug
from everyone's favourite octopus.
Let's get to the Snug!"

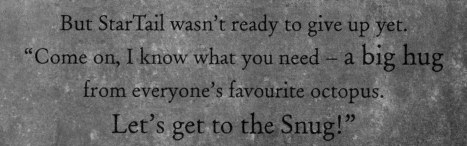

The Snug was home to Cariad, a great big hug of an octopus with enough love in her two hearts for all of Coralia.

"Helloooo," she cooed. "Come in, come in. My guess is that you need a big, squishy octo-cuddle."

She stretched her tentacles around TinyTail and StarTail,
"Now, tell me, my little ones, what's the matter?"
StarTail explained what had happened.

"Hmmm, a problem indeed," said Cariad, softly.
"But remember, it's who you are on the inside that matters most.
It sounds to me like TinyTail could do with a trip to CherryTail's café."

"Of course!" exclaimed StarTail. "Let's go!"

When they arrived at CherryTail's, she had just baked a fresh batch
of her famous cherry buns and everyone wanted one.

When CherryTail heard about TinyTail's missing scale,
she gave her the biggest cherry bun with the most icing.

"Maybe this will help," she said. "It's a whole lot of
love baked in a bun – and this one is just for you!"

The bun looked delicious but
poor TinyTail was feeling far too sad to eat.
Just then, there was a commotion in the ocean . . .

"It's the Travelling Turtles!" squealed
CherryTail. "They're back in town!"

Everyone rushed outside – a visit from the Travelling Turtles was big news.
The turtles always brought back tales and treasures from faraway lands.
This time they were carrying something no one had ever seen before.

"What is it?"
asked StarTail.

Boo and Shine swished around the strange treasure. It had a squidgy,
soft base and a V-shape on top that sparkled with shiny jewels,
shells and sequins. And that was when TinyTail spotted it . . .

"My scale!" she cried. "There's my scale!"

And she was right.
Nestling between the sequins
and jewels was TinyTail's scale.

The problem was that the Travelling
Turtles were using their treasure
as a bed for their babies.

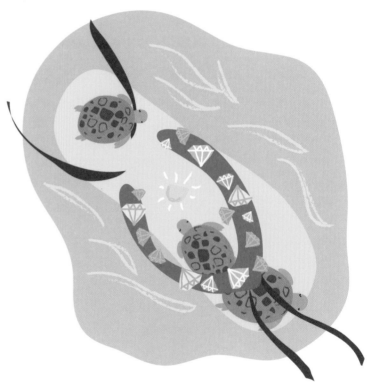

They were definitely not going
to give it up – not even
the tiniest bit of it.

What was TinyTail going to do?

StarTail looked down at her shimmering tail and then did something
truly kind – something only a good friend would do.
She slid off her special star scale . . .

and, with it still sparkling in her hand,
gave it to the turtles in exchange
for TinyTail's lost scale!

"Thank you! Oh thank you!" said TinyTail, overjoyed.
She placed the scale carefully back in her bag.
"But what about your beautiful scale?"

"Remember what Cariad said?" StarTail smiled.
"It's what's inside that really matters."

That night, TinyTail hung her bag under the lantern outside her pod.

Then she snuggled down in her hammock and drifted off to sleep, dreaming of fun times and friends.

The next morning, TinyTail and Boo swooshed eagerly out of the pod. When they opened the bag, they found not one, but two sparkly new scales inside – a heart-shaped ruby and a glittering diamond star.

The Scale Fairy had been!

"One for me and one for my best friend," smiled TinyTail. And she rushed off to tell StarTail the good news!

StarTail was thrilled! Her new scale was even sparklier than
the one she had before. She hugged TinyTail tightly.
Then with a swish and a flick . . .

the two friends set off together on another FurFin adventure.

For Effy and Charlie – A.R.

For Lola – A.B.

BLOOMSBURY CHILDREN'S BOOKS
Bloomsbury Publishing Plc
50 Bedford Square, London, WC1B 3DP, UK

BLOOMSBURY, BLOOMSBURY CHILDREN'S BOOKS and the Diana logo are trademarks of Bloomsbury Publishing Plc

First published in Great Britain 2019 by Bloomsbury Publishing Plc
Text copyright © Bloomsbury Publishing Plc, 2019
Illustrations copyright © Aless Baylis, 2019

Aless Baylis has asserted her right under the Copyright, Designs and Patents Act, 1988, to be identified as Illustrator of this work

A catalogue record for this book is available from the British Library

ISBN: PB: 978-1-4088-9784-3

2 4 6 8 10 9 7 5 3 1 (paperback)

Printed in China by Leo Paper Products, Heshan, Guangdong
All papers used by Bloomsbury Publishing Plc are natural, recyclable products from wood grown in well managed forests.
The manufacturing processes conform to the environmental regulations of the country of origin

To find out more about our authors and books visit www.bloomsbury.com and sign up for our newsletters

See you again soon!

The End